CW01509285

Sherlock Holmes and the
Air Fryer of Doom

ABOUT THE AUTHOR

Bruno Vincent is the author of more than thirty books, which have been translated into fifteen languages. He is best known for the Enid Blyton for Grown Ups series (in which he introduced the Famous Five to the perils of modern life), ten of which were *Sunday Times* bestsellers. He has contributed to serious works about the history of poetry and literature, but has also written humorous books in the voices of Charles Dickens, Prince Harry and Danger Mouse, as well as his own collections of horror stories for children, *Grisly Tales from Tumblewater* and *School for Villains*.

Sherlock Holmes and the Air Fryer of Doom

BRUNO VINCENT

PENGUIN
VIKING

VIKING

UK | USA | Canada | Ireland | Australia
India | New Zealand | South Africa

Viking is part of the Penguin Random House group of companies
whose addresses can be found at global.penguinrandomhouse.com.

Penguin Random House UK,
One Embassy Gardens, 8 Viaduct Gardens, London SW11 7BW

penguin.co.uk
global.penguinrandomhouse.com

First published 2024
001

Set in 12.5/14.75pt Garamond MT Std
Typeset by Jouve (UK), Milton Keynes
Printed and bound in Great Britain by Clays Ltd, Elcograf S.p.A.

The authorized representative in the EEA is Penguin Random House Ireland,
Morrison Chambers, 32 Nassau Street, Dublin D02 YH68

A CIP catalogue record for this book is available from the British Library

ISBN: 978–0–241–72144–5

Penguin Random House is committed to a
sustainable future for our business, our readers
and our planet. This book is made from Forest
Stewardship Council® certified paper.

I

Placing two slips of paper inside the hat, I held it out to Sherlock Holmes. 'You go first,' I said quietly.

Holmes tutted and sighed. 'Must I?' he said.

'Oh, don't spoil this for me, Holmes!' I remonstrated. 'You know how I enjoy it.'

He flared his nostrils and, fishing out a piece of paper, unfolded it and read the contents.

'Well,' he said. 'What a devastating surprise. I shall place an order for those absurdly coarse woollen socks that you seem to enjoy, and on my own part shall look forward to receiving another moustache comb for my collection.'

'Don't ruin it!' I said, clapping my hands over my ears. 'The fun's in the mystery!'

'Really, Watson, I think at least *three* people are required to make an even serviceable "secret Santa".'

'It's these harmless little traditions that make Christmas so fun. The brandy butter, the brightly coloured jumpers . . . the bumper edition of the *Radio Times*!'

'I see you are reassured by all this pageantry,' Holmes said. 'But that doesn't mean I shall be wearing one of those gaudy jumpers. And you're *not* to put tinsel in my pipe again this year.'

'You don't smoke it . . .'

'That is by the by. It aids concentration. As for the not-so-secret Santa, why mayn't we include Mrs Hudson?'

'She is off to look after her sister in North Wales,' I explained, 'who is recovering after having her "legs done".'

'Her "legs done"? What does this mean?'

'I did not ask.'

'Quite right,' agreed Holmes. 'It is better that some mysteries remain unsolved.'

'But – ah, indeed, legs: it brings me to the subject of the festive dinner. What sort of roasted bird might we like, do you think?'

'Nothing for me. A tin of tomato soup will do as well as anything.'

'Holmes! But it's Christmas dinner! The season of merriment and goodwill!'

'I've said it before, Watson, you have a touchingly naive view of human nature. Look at this lonely city! The empty spectacle of Christmas – with its fakery of bright lights and jingling bells – alleviates none of the evil that lurks in its dark purlieus. A sham which empties the pockets of the poor, encourages inebriation . . .'

I looked at him aghast, but Holmes was lost in a reverie, staring gloomily from his customary spot by the window. He could not be interrupted when moods like this took control of him.

'Christmas simply intensifies the merciless battle of a dog-eat-dog world, heaps more misery upon the miserable – and leaves the scent of blood in the air, Watson!'

'I swear the Oxford Street Christmas Lights get more and more over-the-top every year.'

2

'Holmes, I must protest!' I said. 'This is most unlike you. What has caused this sudden despondency? And besides, there is no need for anyone to eat dog. I have had a good look at some festive recipes and – after rejecting Heston Blumenthal's partridge cooked in ice cream and dynamite – was thinking perhaps goose this year . . .'

'Ah, Watson!' he said, turning and flashing me a rueful grin. 'Forgive me. It is I who is the goose. A strange mood overtakes me at this time of year when the "holidays", as our American cousins call them, come into view, and I perceive the dreaded spectacle that is Black Friday.'

I nodded, glad that Holmes's dark mood seemed to have abated. 'It is an undignified spectacle of course,' I said. 'Consumerism red in tooth and claw, as you say. But why should it affect you so strongly, my dear friend?'

'Consumerism?' he asked, distracted.

'The sales, the discounts, the endless advertisements, and the pressure on poor families to spend beyond their means . . .' I broke off, for he was giving me one of his stiffest stares, equal parts bafflement and scorn.

'I have no idea what *you* are blathering about,' he said. 'I am talking about the one case which has stretched on year after year, and which I have singularly failed to solve. It frustrates me and makes me doubt – not just my own powers, but that a great darkness holds sway in this mighty city of ours.'

'Surely I have never heard you mention this before?' I asked.

'I have kept this one to myself. And brooded upon it. Each year, regularly as clockwork, it happens – on the same day. A brutal and completely inexplicable murder . . .'

3

'Tell me more!' I said, taking out my book and making some discreet notes. 'I am listening.'

'It started three years ago,' said my friend. 'A man run down in Russell Square while crossing the road.'

'Deliberately run down?'

'I believe so,' said Holmes. 'A year later to the day, another man pushed in front of a tube train at South Kensington station. The following year – nothing.'

'Ah,' I said. It seemed to me that either my friend the famous consulting detective was holding something back, or that he was starting to see connections for which there was no evidence.

'On the day itself – nothing. But ten days later, a body washed up at Limehouse. And the man reported missing on the sixth of December. What connects these cases?'

'Something, I hope?' I said.

'Indeed. Each of the victims *was dressed as Santa Claus.*'

He said this with a magnificent flourish, turning to look at me triumphantly. I felt unable to supply the requisite reaction, and looked on with puzzled sympathy.

'Don't you see it?' he asked.

'I see an *unfortunate* series of ... perhaps ... sad coincidences?'

Holmes came and stood over me, clearly displeased. He looked over my shoulder into my notebook. I had written: potatoes, carrots, cabbage, cranberry sauce, stuffing, peas ...

'No sprouts?'

'Oh Holmes, you know the effect they have on you.'

'But I like sprouts!'

'I'm afraid I do *not* like you liking them. And as I'm doing the shopping, they are off the list.'

He huffed. 'Who's the spoilsport now,' he muttered. 'And who also fails to see what's as plain as the nose on his face – the fact that the sixth of December is the feast day of Saint Nicholas? We have a Santa serial killer on our hands, do you not admit that?'

4

Again, I found myself unable to give Holmes the outburst of astonishment and admiration he clearly considered his just desserts. Which reminded me . . .

'Christmas pudding and brandy butter from Fortnum's again this year?'

'Yes, yes, fine,' he said. 'Although honestly I'm as indifferent to Christmas pudding as you are to my brilliant deductions. Don't you *see*? There's someone out there, getting away with it. And it's the sixth of December today!'

'Why aren't you out investigating, then?' I asked. It was helpful to me when planning festive occasions if Holmes could be out of the house.

A difficulty had arisen in our affairs in recent times – or perhaps I should say there always had been one, but that it had become highlighted and worsened by the rising cost of living. The wonderful detective who all the world admired, also admired himself quite as much, and was too proud most of the time either to demand payment for his investigations or (perhaps more to the point) to chase said payment when it had been promised but was not forthcoming.

There was no question that the great man ought to continue to live in the style to which he had become accustomed. But to facilitate matters, some discreet alterations had to be made. The Fortnum's Christmas pudding, for instance, had been substituted years earlier for a Tesco one. Other small replacements abounded: the 'Harvey Nichols' crackers were from Aldi and the 'Neal's Yard' Stilton from Morrisons.

All that was needed was a brief window of time so that he wouldn't see me entering 221B Baker Street lugging supermarket shopping bags.

But he was not to be encouraged to go out.

'I can't charge around investigating where I haven't been asked,' he said. 'I am a private detective, not a citizen activist. What I need to get involved is for someone to knock on that door, and come in and say, "Please Mr Holmes, I beg you to investigate this case for me."'

There came at that precise moment a knock exactly as he had described. He and I both jumped, and looked at each other, and begged the person to come in.

The door opened and a supremely elegant and expensively dressed lady of about sixty entered. She was soft-spoken and demure, but clearly in emotional turmoil.

'Mr Holmes?' she inquired. He nodded. 'I am desperate for your help. Something terrible has happened. Can you come and look into the matter at once?'

Holmes had taken up his pipe, which he always did in moments of excitement, and bit the mouthpiece to conceal his grin. He turned to me.

'You see, Watson?' he said. 'Exactly like that.'

'Allow me to introduce you to Mr Percival,' said Holmes,
'who is perfectly convinced that he has turned into a chair.'

5

Our guest ushered us to a waiting black cab, which set off at once for Mayfair. I felt I faintly recognized her, which was not at all impossible, as we soon learned she was a former stage and film actress who occasionally adorned the society columns of the newspapers. Her name was Lady Desdemona Winterbourne, and she was the wife of the well-known industrialist Lord Winterbourne.

'I've made such a terrible mistake,' she said, as the cab swept around a corner, narrowly avoiding an illuminated rickshaw, its speakers thumping with obnoxiously loud music. The dark December sky was suddenly filled by Oxford Street's Christmas lights, glittering down at us. 'I can't forgive myself – I feel so humiliated, so . . .'

'Madam,' said Holmes. 'We can only help you, and you only help yourself, by a strict explanation of the facts of the case. Stick to those, and we shall do all in our power.'

'Yes,' she said. 'Yes, of course. Oh dear. What will he say . . .'

'Your husband?' Holmes asked. She nodded, and seemed close to tears.

'Take deep breaths,' I advised her.

She did so, looking out of the window at the

thousands of shoppers streaming past. Then her actor's training asserted itself, and over the course of a dozen minutes, the story spilled out.

'My husband has been under some enormous stress. I do not know what it is – he always keeps his business affairs close to his chest. But he has not been himself. He is upset. Naturally this is a very private matter, you understand . . .'

'Our discretion is absolutely assured,' said Holmes, and I could see from the corner of my eye he was so excited by the prospects of the case he was nearly biting through the stem of his unlit meerschaum.

Lady Desdemona explained that, while regarding her husband's distress with a sense of helplessness, she had overheard him remark in an unguarded moment that all would be well with him, if he could just hold the 'Baghdad Beryl' in his hand.

'Baghdad Beryl – wasn't she one of your consorts in the old days, Watson?' Holmes asked.

'Please, Holmes!' I said.

6

'Now tell us,' I said reassuringly. 'This Baghdad Beryl is . . . a precious stone?'

'It is. Its provenance is disputed. It's one of those gems that people are always saying ought to be returned to the country it came from. Which isn't originally Iraq – it was found there, having been formerly looted . . . I forget the details. All I knew was that my husband was obsessed with it, and that I loved him and I wanted him to be happy again . . .'

The cab had slipped from the main London thoroughfares to deposit us in a quiet square of tall mansions, with a private garden in the centre surrounded by cast-iron railings. The festive bustle of the city was instantly forgotten, as though it might be a hundred miles away.

Walking up the stone stops, I half expected the door to be opened by a sober elderly footman, but Lady Winterbourne produced the keys and let us in. Not long afterwards she was pouring tea from a silver tea set in a drawing room of stately magnificence and exquisitely refined taste.

'I never would have thought of it myself,' she said, sitting. 'But you see, we – my husband and I – met this extraordinary man, at some society function. A fundraiser, I think it was. He was very mysterious and . . . well, frankly suspicious. My husband is very active in museum circles, always has been. It's his passion. And I know that sometimes museums are forced to deal with some very nefarious characters in order to secure the items they want to display. It was whispered that this fellow was just such a person . . .

'Well, this gem, the Baghdad Beryl,' she sighed. 'I knew that it had been withdrawn from display. There were rumours it had been stolen, or gone missing. And so I contacted this individual. He was cagey at first but said he *could* get it for me. It was . . .' She broke off, and looked at her surroundings. 'We are not poor,' she said. 'And I had some money left to me. The jewel cost nearly as much as this house. But I knew he wanted it.'

'This man. He brought it here?' Holmes asked.

'No, I met him. I carried it home. I don't suppose he knew where we live but then it's hardly a state secret either.'

'And it's gone missing,' Holmes said baldly.

7

Lady Winterbourne held back a tear and nodded.

Then she led us upstairs, to the bedroom, and showed us a safe set into the wall.

'Your husband wouldn't look in here?'

She shook her head. 'He has his own bank deposit boxes for his precious things – this is for my jewellery. I was going to give it to him at Christmas. What will I do now . . .'

Holmes looked around the room. The windows were secure and fitted on the outside with cast-iron bars to prevent burglary. The bedroom (aside from its expensive furnishings) offered no other points of interest, being spotlessly clean and tidy, and Holmes asked to see the top of the house for possible points of entry.

In an attic room there was a skylight, which was ajar. Holmes examined it closely, peered out at the roof, then turned to look carefully from the back window. Pointing to a garage roof in the rear garden, which overlooked a little mews street, he muttered under his breath to me: 'The memory game, Watson!'

This was a favourite challenge of his, to see if I could manage to spot something he had noticed. I looked carefully, while Lady Desdemona chattered away nervously, as though in denial.

'There's nothing else he wants, or needs . . . What other Christmas present could I buy him . . . what's the latest fad?'

'One of those funny kitchen things,' I said vaguely, remembering a recent conversation I had overheard.

'An air fryer, you mean?' she said. 'Oh, they're marvellous, aren't they? You know, my brother-in-law is a professional chef, and he swears by his . . . Mr Holmes, are you all right?'

Sherlock Holmes was standing stock-still. He held out a hand to her.

'I shall take on this case,' he said. 'And you shall give me the name of this strange gentleman. Fear not, I shall be discreet, and cautious. And now, Watson, would you please answer the telephone which is buzzing so distractingly in your pocket? Unless I'm much mistaken that is a call from Scotland Yard, which means in all likelihood we have another pressing matter to attend to at once!'

8

The marble pillars of the Museum of Great Britain were starkly lit in wintry white and soared above us as we approached.

There was a gaggle of people near the great door, and Sherlock's appearance made a few heads turn. One was that of a bright, intelligent-looking young woman whose face I recognized. She came straight over to us, disconcertingly with a camera crew in tow.

'The famous Sherlock Holmes!' she said ingratiatingly. 'May I ask if you are here to investigate some juicy crime?'

'I'm not at liberty . . .' began Holmes, and I saw at once why he broke off. It was because the woman with the camera crew was proudly adorned (over her jumper) by a white T-shirt with the slogan 'I ♥ old shit!' She was wearing glittery eyeshadow and glistening lipstick, and seemed to exude gleeful curiosity.

This was Akila Jassim, the new female historian who was all over the television – and, I had heard it said, was a star of social media (and in particular Tick Tock), although whether the latter accolade was a good or a bad thing, or a great or a small achievement, was beyond my power to say. She specialized in documentaries celebrating the racier aspects of females in history, which drove many traditional viewers (and Sherlock Holmes in particular) to distraction with their brightly coloured, tabloid treatment of important subjects.

I saw Holmes's spine stiffen as he recognized her.

'I'm gratified to meet you,' he said formally. 'I most enjoyed your series *Cleopatra: History's Biggest Shagger?*'

In response to this insincere compliment, the extraordinary woman reached out and actually *punched Sherlock Holmes on the arm*. Both he and I looked down at her fist as it retreated, and she giggled girlishly.

'No you didn't, you hated it,' she said. 'Don't kid a kidder! Okay, Sally, turn the camera off, I'm not trying to do a "gotcha" on Mr Holmes here. Forgive me – I'm a massive fan. Hope you're here for something fun or interesting.' Then she leant in confidentially. 'There are rumours round here that there's been some sort of crime inside. Don't suppose you can tell me what?'

'I am here to be admitted as one of the eldest exhibits,' said Sherlock Holmes, nodding with a slight smile. She grinned brilliantly back at him. I thought she'd punch him again, perhaps on the chin this time, but instead she reiterated what an enormous fan of his she was, and waved enthusiastically as we both retreated.

'Mr Holmes!' said a voice, and a friendly figure came forward. He was shortish, and not un-plump, and with his snowy curling beard and bubbly demeanour he made us both feel welcome at once.

Behind him trailed a police detective of our acquaintance, Inspector Kanchelsky, a rather severe and humourless person of about sixty who disapproved of private investigators in general, and Sherlock in particular (and, one sometimes got the impression, all men and almost all women as well). She was coldly formal.

'My name is Sir Gerald Huntingdon,' said our friendly host. 'I'm the museum's curator. We are so glad you could come.'

Kanchelsky simply nodded a curt greeting as we were guided through the throng of people, mostly museum employees who seemed puzzled and inconvenienced to be locked out of their place of work in the middle of a busy day.

We were taken beyond a police cordon and inside, up some steps and into the Grand Exhibition Room. Around the walls were arrayed tall tablets covered in a beautiful cuneiform script, and at the centre of the room what appeared to be a large stone altar had been erected.

'This is our grand new exhibition,' said Sir Gerald. 'It's all still under wraps. Hasn't even been announced – we are looking at some amazing new discoveries from Asia Minor that shed light on the Achaemenid Empire. It is, quite unjustly, one of the least examined of ancient civilizations . . .'

Many exhibits were still being moved into place, and lights and electric cables were scattered around. The arrangement of the last few details of the exhibition had clearly been cut short.

'I don't think this is a good idea, getting Holmes in here,' said Kanchelsky. 'But I have to admit you always

'Mr Holmes, welcome to the Museum of Great Britain –
which definitely is not the British Museum, because I don't
want to get into the shit with any lawyers.'

have ideas when we are faced with something weird,
inexplicable or disturbing. And there's no better
description for what we're looking at . . .'

'This morning, cleaners came to open up the space,'
said Sir Gerald. 'Look what they found.' He pointed.

The altar at the centre of the room had four tall stone needles around it, one in each corner, presumably for some ceremonial purpose. Or rather – three. For one of them had fallen. As we came closer, I heard Sherlock whistle under his breath.

'What do you make of this, Watson?' he said quietly.

'Good grief!' I let out, before I could suitably control myself.

Beneath the fourth of the stone needles, surrounded by scene-of-crime officers and apparently crushed to death, was a human figure, possibly a man's.

He was wearing a very recognizable red-and-white costume.

'What do you say to my Santa serial killer theory now?' Holmes asked, triumphantly.

9

Soon afterwards we were in the curator's office, quizzing him on the details that had been gathered so far.

'This person,' said Sir Gerald, 'is not known to me. I think he broke in during the night.'

'There should be footage on the CCTV,' I said.

'Sadly not,' said Sir Gerald. 'It's very odd, but there was a power cut in the middle of the night and all the cameras went out.'

'We think the victim caused the outage,' said Kanchelsky from the corner of the room, 'to hide his crime.'

'Interesting, isn't it,' said Holmes. 'We are in a quandary whether to call him the victim or the culprit, are we not? I wonder what he was trying to do?'

'Vandalism?' Kanchelsky suggested. 'Or are Fathers 4 Justice active at the moment?'

'But why not wait for the exhibition to open, and vandalize it then, as others have memorably done with various famous artworks?' asked Holmes. 'I wonder if there was any grudge against the exhibition itself, or museums in general – against the theft of cultural artefacts . . .'

'Out of the question,' said the curator sharply. Then he smiled at me. 'It had not been announced, there was no way of his knowing what we had in there.'

I noticed how swiftly his beaming smile returned, after his sharp words: a force of will, to suppress the evidence of his feelings. Meanwhile Holmes was explaining his findings.

'I examined the rock which fell,' he said, 'and it's hard to be sure but it seems to me that it was definitely pushed. It was very well secured in place, and for it to fall at such a moment as to land on someone is too much of a coincidence. There are some marks on the surface but it's hard to be conclusive.'

'Your theories are always interesting and often helpful,' Kanchelsky conceded, almost through gritted teeth, 'and I hope you'll share any thoughts with me in the coming days?'

Holmes promised that he would, and he was uncharacteristically quiet on the walk home, adding up certainties and probabilities, making his infinite tiny calculations, while I considered what I (or rather, Secret Santa) was to get him for Christmas.

His silence lasted until we entered our Baker Street apartments, when he began by saying, 'There are many interesting points to discuss, Wats—'

He broke off, and stood still and alert.

'Oh, turn on the light by all means, I didn't mean to startle you,' said a voice from the chair in the corner of the room.

'Lord Winterbourne, I presume?' said Holmes coldly.

The man in the chair under the window was lean and healthy, aged perhaps just past seventy and with a powerful expression and manner that betrayed complete self-possession and control. He had his legs crossed and was examining us with mild interest, but I noticed that the foot of the leg crossed over his knee tapped briskly and unconsciously, as though he was under considerable pressure.

'Forgive my intruding,' he said. 'Your housekeeper let me in; I said I was a client of yours.'

'Mrs Hudson is my *landlady*,' Holmes corrected him.

'And you wish to assure yourself that we will keep your wife's actions absolutely secret,' I said, suddenly divining the purpose of his visit. 'I assure you, you have nothing to worry about!'

Holmes turned on me with the severest expression of disapproval.

'My what?' Lord Winterbourne asked. 'What on earth do you know about my wife?'

'Watson, busy yourself getting a drink for our guest!' I'd hardly ever heard him speak to me more sharply, and I saw by the flexing of the muscles around his eyes that he was sincerely furious with me.

'What's that man talking about?' asked the peer of the realm.

'Ignore my idiot cousin,' said Holmes, at once deducing that Lord Winterbourne was far too eminent and famous to be aware of such an insignificant personage as myself. 'I look after him on Friday afternoons as a favour for my family. You can speak freely in front of him, he will remember nothing.'

'I wish to employ you to investigate a crime,' said Lord Winterbourne. 'I have recently invested a large amount of money in the private purchase of a very valuable piece of jewellery.' He paused, and seemed to notice his own tapping foot. He rested a hand on it to stop it, and mastered whatever emotion he was experiencing. 'The jewel has gone missing. Thank you.'

His last words were in response to my handing him a brandy and soda.

'You came by this jewel via unorthodox means,' said Holmes.

'I did. An unfortunate lapse of judgement. How did you know?'

'Otherwise it would simply be a matter for the insurance company,' said Holmes. 'What can you tell me about this piece? And where was it taken from?'

'It is called the Lucknow Teardrop. It is very ancient, and extremely expensive. Worse, I don't understand how anyone knew I had it.'

'Except the person who sold it to you,' suggested Holmes.

'Naturally,' said Lord Winterbourne.

'And your girlfriend, who asked you for it.'

For the first time, this powerful man seemed disarranged in his person. He sat up as though he'd received an electric shock, but regained his composure quickly. He regarded Holmes with hostility and reluctant interest.

'What makes you say that?' he asked.

'Well, it could have been a boyfriend,' Holmes admitted. 'But no one so eminent and with so much to lose as yourself would ever make such a rash gesture except under the pressure of secrecy, it seems to me.'

Lord Winterbourne's mouth creased with displeasure. 'The jewel was delivered to me, I carried it to my place of work, which is an office in Whitehall, and discovered when I got there that I had been expertly pickpocketed.'

'Don't think I'm being frivolous,' said Holmes. 'But did you run into someone – bump into, I mean – in a Santa Claus costume, during your journey?'

A look of sheer annoyance crossed Lord Winterbourne's face, as of one who suddenly realizes he has been wasting his precious time. He reached for his coat and then, as he stood, an extraordinary change overcame him. He looked at Holmes with open astonishment.

'I took the tube to St James's Park. There was a drunken party on the platform, being rowdy. I did my best to avoid them, but yes – I got jostled. And damn it to hell, there *was* someone dressed as Father Christmas!'

Our superior and disagreeable guest had little else to tell. He had only held the precious stone in his possession for less than an hour, all told. He furnished Holmes with the name of the broker who had sold him the item. He insisted on total discretion, requested regular updates, cast a disapproving (or was it sympathetic?) glance in my direction, and left.

Holmes threw himself onto the chaise longue, gazed up at the ceiling and sighed.

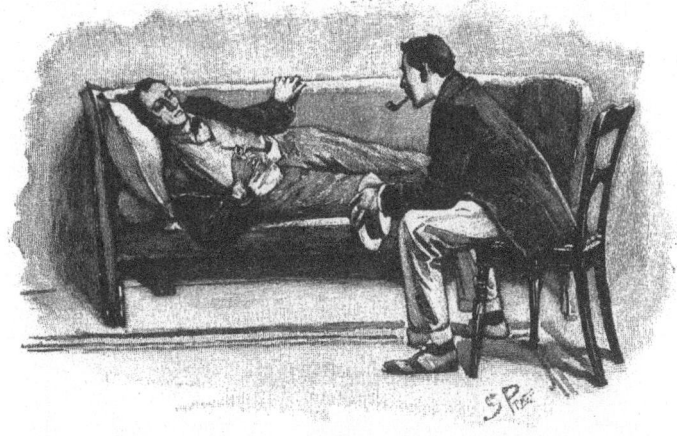

'It is a posture I've adopted to make me look more authoritative and respectable – I got the inspiration from that thoroughly impressive gentleman Mr Rees-Mogg.'

'Oh for a pipe, or a couple of dozen cigarettes,' he said. 'This thing starts to take shape! Now I need to think, and let it all come together . . .'

'Why not go for a nice refreshing walk,' I said. 'Clear your head? I daresay you haven't got your ten thousand steps in yet . . .'

'Rubbish. Go for a walk? Clear my head? That is the last thing I need to do. Everything's in there, I just need to sort through the facts! Some form of mental exercise is needed. Which is of course aided by physical exercise. Yes. That's it. Let's go for a walk, Watson!' He jumped up and pulled on his coat.

'I just suggested you do that very thing . . .' I said.

'Stop dawdling, cousin of mine, and put your coat on. We're going out! We've an appointment with a deeply sinister purveyor of stolen goods!'

When in a terrible mood, Sherlock Holmes could be quite impossible to deal with. When in a stimulated and jubilant frame of mind, he was only a fraction better. Unable to resist, I followed him into the street, where he glided with ease through the crammed throng while with frustration I bumbled and bumped against seemingly every tourist in the capital.

At last we passed beyond the shopping district and the West End, crossed the old Fleet river, and drifted towards the parts of the city where the shadier types of business dealings were conducted in insalubrious dens of crime.

It had been our ill luck to visit many such a one on former occasions, and Holmes had always advised me to bring my revolver. This was no longer open to us, as I had allowed my licence to lapse after an incident where it had gone off while I was cleaning it and had euthanized a neighbour's prize parakeet.

Instead, my grip tightened around the cosh in my side pocket as I envisaged a tense exchange in a dingy, malodorous underground room, surrounded by barrels of illicit merchandise.

I was still nerving myself to this confrontation when the great detective stopped and I nearly bumped into him.

'Here we are then,' he said, looking up. We were in front of a clean, bright hotel entirely walled with glass, and with a soft cream interior and fittings that gave the impression more of a futuristic airport lounge than an East End dive.

The door was not immediately apparent, but as Holmes approached, two giant panels of glass slid noiselessly apart to admit us, and a courteous and demure receptionist asked if he could help us.

'A room for the night, gentlemen?' he asked, then looked between us. 'Or the hour?'

'I have an appointment with one of your guests,' said Holmes, giving the name, as I retreated in flustered embarrassment to examine the art on the walls.

A hushed telephone conversation followed, after which we were invited to step into the lift. Coming out on the eighth floor, we walked along plush silent carpets to a room, where a muscle-clad giant of a man in a neat black suit, with a discreet radio piece in one ear, opened the door for us.

Within was a palatial suite. In its centre was a desk, across which a rather ordinary-looking man of middle years regarded us suspiciously.

'Please be sitting,' he said, in an Eastern European accent which I struggled to place. He indicated the chairs in front of his desk with a minimal gesture.

'Nice to meet you!' said Holmes heartily. 'I am—'

'I know who you are, Mr Holmes,' said the man. 'My name is Zabkus.'

'Excellent! No need for introductions. I'm most glad

you accepted my request for an interview, as I am here on a matter of great delicacy.'

I was grateful that Holmes had taken charge of the conversation, as I was much distracted by two further specimens of the sport of bodybuilding, who loomed behind the man at the desk. They were somehow even larger than the one who had greeted us outside, and so statuesque that they seemed almost to creak within their ill-fitting suits, one bearing a esoteric design which stretched up his neck like a ritualistic warrior tattoo.

'Everything I do is a matter of great delicacy,' said Zabkus softly. 'But I am afraid you will be disappointed, Mr Holmes, and I advise you to leave at once – if you value your safety.'

13

'Come, come,' said Holmes, chuckling. 'There's no need for such threats, especially at this time of year. We can all conduct our business quickly and allow you to get back to something more conducive to the festive spirit, like carol singing, handing out alms to the needy and so forth! I trust your boss is getting you something good this year?' he said, addressing the heavies.

'An air fryer,' said the giant on the left.

'Is that all?' said Holmes. 'I'm sure his pockets must stretch deeper . . .'

'It's what we requested,' said the goliath on the right, who had a surprisingly gentle voice and (like his fellow) a melodious Midlands lilt. 'Healthier, but still delicious. Cauliflower goujons come up a treat . . .' He made a chef's-kiss hand gesture.

'And Hasselback sprouts,' said his colleague on the left, enthusiastically.

'You see, Watson? Everyone adores sprouts!' said Holmes.

'Please, Holmes, no . . .' I said.

'Enough of this,' said Zabkus. 'I am afraid you wish to speak to me about some business I did with Lord Winterbourne.'

'Yes,' said Holmes. 'And Lady Winterbourne, in fact.

I'm sorry to say you have two very unhappy customers, both of whose – ah, merchandise – vanished within twenty-four hours of your delivering it. You are the only link between the two.'

'It is, ah . . .' Zabkus stopped. He was clearly displeased, but equally saw that the evidence was bad against him. His severe face simply went still for a moment as he looked between us. 'Do not be suggesting my involvement. I do nothing wrong.'

'Except supplying stolen jewels in the first place,' suggested Holmes in a cheerful tone. At this, Zabkus's expressionless face somehow drained even further of expression, and I began to feel uncomfortable, checking over my shoulder the distance to the door and putting my hand to the cosh in my pocket.

'You have about ten seconds before I lose my temper,' said Zabkus. The men behind him stirred.

'It's perfectly simple,' said Holmes. 'If you tell me how and from whom you got those jewels, I shall help clear this matter up for all involved.'

'Impossible,' said Zabkus. 'Because I myself do not know.'

14

'Most unfortunate,' said Holmes, frowning.

'This is very exceptional vendor, from who I am buying,' said Zabkus. He threaded his fingers together in front of him, and then looked at them as distantly as though they were an exotic stick insect, while he spoke. It seemed to be physically painful to him, to reveal anything about his business.

'I am told when an item is available, via anonymous communication. I find buyer. I sell. I receive goods also anonymously. I know nothing more than this.'

Holmes was quite unsatisfied. 'I appreciate you don't want to damage your own business by letting someone steal the items . . . That would be quite foolish.'

'Is correct,' said Zabkus softly.

'Can I actually see the said items? My clients were unable to show me them.'

Zabkus leant back in his chair and looked down his nose at both of us. Then he fished in his pocket and took out a mobile device. Unlocking it, he stood and came round his desk, then held it out for Holmes to see. I shifted my chair closer to get a look as well.

'Of course I am able to complete Wordle in two moves,
Watson – but not with you two staring over my shoulder.'

'Let me ... wait, my glasses, excuse me ...
Ah, now – how do I expand this photograph? Oh
dear!'

Holmes fumbled the device as he tried to manipulate
the image, and it fell to the floor. He pounced on it and
made a series of apologies while Zabkus looked on
with a foreboding expression, then snatched it back as
soon as he could.

'Yes, thank you – most interesting pieces. We shall
go now.'

'That is good idea,' said Zabkus. 'I trust you will not be back.'

'Come, Watson. Most interesting to have met you all. I hope the air fryers bring you health and many delicious meals in the new year, gentlemen!'

It is so often the way with these investigations of ours, that everything happens at once and then, all of a sudden – nothing at all. So it proved in the two cases of the missing jewels and the death of the museum burgler in the Father Christmas costume.

My friend, the famous sleuth, suddenly vanished like a bloodhound into a thick wood. No sign of him was seen or heard for many days, which became a week and then two weeks.

The season marched on. Christmas cards gathered on the mantelpiece like snow. I sent out the annual round-robin letter to our list of acquaintances (including several addresses whose first lines began 'HMP', Holmes having maintained correspondence with a surprising number of those he had put in prison). I pinned some mistletoe to the corner of the ceiling above a bookcase, where it could not occasion any awkwardness, and dug out the jolly Christmas jumpers from the box in the attic, laying one out on Holmes's bed (with little expectation that he would wear it). A new and even more baffling John Lewis advert appeared, and a novelty song sprang into the charts, in the hope of being Christmas number one.

At the back of my mind was the knowledge that

Sherlock Holmes had always until now resurfaced, whether slinking back in a spirit of despair and doldrums, or in the electric excitement of the final moments of a hunt.

Yet of course I had to spend every day in the knowledge that this might be the time when his luck ran out, that I would be called to some desperate place to find he had fallen foul of some gang of ne'er-do-wells, or failed to make some acrobatic leap between rooftops. For the thousandth time my heart darkened as I was forced to make mental preparations for such a dreadful event, and I cursed being left so thoroughly in the dark.

During this testing period I managed to complete my festive preparations. It only remained for me to purchase a secret Santa gift for perhaps the most particular and difficult-to-please man in Christendom.

Thus I was standing outside an exclusive gentleman's outfitters examining umbrellas and walking sticks, and wondering what on earth I could purchase, when I found myself accosted by a youth in a hoodie wearing the yellow tabard of a charity worker.

'May I talk to you for a moment about children in poverty?' he asked.

'Ah, you see – I'm afraid I must—'

'I'm sure you don't want to allow children to be unable to eat at Christmas?' he said.

'No indeed, but . . . I already donate . . . I'm late for a . . .'

The youth smiled ingratiatingly at me and said he would take up just one moment of my time. Realizing I could not squeeze past him without being decidedly rude, with a feeling of defeat I acceded to his request.

'What would you say,' said the charity worker, all broad smiles, 'if I said you were a selfish old codger who just wants to keep his own ill-gotten money stuffed in his pockets and not lift a finger to help people in terrible need?'

'I beg your pardon!' I said. 'Why, I've never—'

'Okay, Boomer.' He grinned. 'Now, how about a spot of lunch?'

My heart leapt and rolled over, and I took a deep breath. 'Holmes!' I gasped. 'Where the blazes have you been? And why must you always accost me in this fashion?'

'Oh, get over it, grandad,' Holmes said, pushing back the hood. 'My finest disguise yet, is it not? Also I've collected over a dozen direct debits for Save the Children today. What have you done for the good of mankind in the same period, Watson?'

My emotions having got the better of me, I declined to reply as we walked along, while Holmes updated me about his progress.

'Much has been learned, Watson. Much has been revealed. Much shall be told!'

16

I perceived he was in one of his better moods. I took notice of the pretty dancing lights stretching across Charing Cross Road, looked in through a bookshop window and tossed a coin to a beggar. When in this humour Holmes needed no encouragement from me – indeed, he could not be stopped.

'I say,' he said, dawdling outside Foyles, 'look at all these books with "air fryer" in the title. I pity the poor author, trying to get noticed among this maelstrom!'

'It serves them right for following a transient fashion, Holmes,' said I.

'An uncharacteristically ungenerous comment, surely, my dear Watson?' he asked teasingly.

'I speak as an author of some experience,' I replied, rather stiffly.

I allowed his flow of drollery to continue until we were back at Baker Street, where, while Holmes changed out of his disguise, I flicked on the television.

'At this point,' said a familiar jaunty voice, 'Queen Victoria must have been like, OMG. It was a real WTF moment . . .'

'Not that appalling woman again,' said Holmes from behind a screen. 'What's her name?'

'Akila Jassim,' I said, watching as the young woman

walked in front of Blenheim Palace in a full-sized Victorian crinoline, whipping the air with a riding crop and winking at the camera.

'It was at this point,' she was saying, 'that things were about to get seriously sexy in the House of Hanover. Or should I say, House of Legover . . .'

'I confess I find her rather entertaining, Holmes . . .'

'But it's this ghastly dumbing-down! What's this documentary called?'

I checked the schedule. 'Um, *Queen Victoria: Empress of the Bedroom.*'

'I mean, really! Why can't they present history with its due sober seriousness?'

'Beats me, Holmes.'

'Looks like you'd like *her* to beat you with that riding crop, the way you're goggling at the box. Enough of this pornography, Watson, I'm famished. To lunch!'

'*1,001 Air Fryer Recipes to Make Before You Die?*' sighed
Holmes. 'I say, aren't they rather scraping the barrel with
that book series?'

17

In short order we were at a favoured lunching venue, with menus in front of us.

'Tell me,' Holmes asked the waiter. 'Have any of these dishes been prepared with one of these "air fryers" I keep hearing so much about?'

'No, sir,' said the waiter. 'In fact, Chef doesn't allow the use of those words on the premises.'

'Marvellous!' said Holmes, turning to me. 'Then hopefully we are safe from those man-mountains who threatened to pull our heads off last time we were together. Now, I think I owe you an explanation . . .'

'I shall say you do,' I said hotly. 'All this dashing about and being mysterious. It's no good for my blood pressure!'

'Oh, quieten down, and wait till you hear what I found. Your little ticker will be loping along at a relaxed speed when you see what progress I've made. Now, we were drawn into two cases in a single day. Was it a coincidence?'

'Surely, Holmes! I can't see any connection.'

'Hmm,' he said, crunching into the end of a bread-stick. 'I'm not so sure. Coincidences exist of course, but there are some subtle connections. Lord Winterbourne has all his life been connected with the museum fraternity. It is *his passion*, his wife said.'

'My heart goes out to poor Lady Winterbourne,' I said sorrowfully.

'Mine too, Watson. Considering what a heartless scoundrel she's married to. If there's anyone in this case I want to protect, it is her. She risked everything to get hold of a jewel that is very precious to her husband. He did the same – for very different, or perhaps I mean decidedly similar, motivations. He has been under a lot of pressure, "and not himself". So, what does this mean? You remember the game of memory I challenged you to?'

'I do!' I said. 'Now, I believe you spotted something on the garage roof which the burglar almost certainly climbed to gain access to the Winterbourne residence.'

'Correct.'

'There were . . . let me see . . . some coils of wire. A few broken laths of wood. A mouldy tennis ball . . .'

'Very good, Watson, but what else?'

'By Jove, yes – a beer can! Of what make? And what does it tell us?'

'Carlsberg,' said Holmes. 'A Pilsner beer brewed for the undemanding drinker. It tells us the English hooligan is alive and well and throwing refuse in the mews streets of Mayfair. But little else. No, you've missed one other thing.'

'I can't quite recall . . .' It was frustrating, after Holmes had taught me so painstakingly to emulate his photographic memory. But I drew a blank, until: 'Wait! A sock?'

'What colour?'

I thought, and visualized the scene again. 'Red!' I said. 'With a white bit at the end . . . but wait!'

'You've got it,' said Holmes. 'It was grubby and dis-coloured by rain, and curled up in one corner. But unless I'm very much mistaken, it was not a sock, but a discarded Santa hat!'

18

'I've got a foie gras and a dozen oysters,' said the waiter.

'Both for me,' said Holmes. 'The green salad's for Watson over there . . .'

'You know, Holmes,' I said, as I watched him tuck in, 'perhaps there is something in this air fryer business. After all, much healthier, you know . . .'

'If there is a certain secret Santa listening in to this conversation,' Holmes said through a mouthful of duck liver, 'I do *not* want a blessed . . .' He lowered his voice. '. . . *A.F.* Watch your language, Watson, or you'll have us thrown out by an angry chef. But speaking of Santas, it seems to me we now do have some kind of connection. Vague, yes – inscrutable for the time being. But there's something there.'

'Tell me then,' I said, taking up a forkful of rather bare salad leaves, 'what have you been doing these past two weeks?'

'Ah! Yes. We should discuss the mysterious Zabkus. What did you make of *him*?' So saying, Holmes fixed my eyes with an intent stare while holding out his wine glass for a hovering waiter to refill.

'A dangerous man, I should say – from a dangerous world. Not one to be trifled with!'

'So he wanted you to believe. Trying rather too hard, if you ask me. There were a plethora of clues pointing to his real identity. Did you not notice his accent?'

'Russian,' I said. But then reconsidered. 'Or perhaps Polish? Although . . .'

'Yes, now you think about it you start to notice his accent slid all the way across Eastern Europe and back like a drunken *Orient Express*. Not convincing in the slightest. Which leads me to believe his own accent is very recognizable. Probably from one of those parts of England where accents change every twenty miles or so and can be identified by the eagle-eared to quite a narrow geographical location.'

'A very astute observation,' I admitted, as we were served our mains – plain omelette for me, steak for Holmes.

'I should say – parts of Lancashire or the West Midlands qualify,' Holmes mused. 'Then did you see the neck tattoo on one of his gorillas?'

'A warlike decoration, it seemed to me.'

'Perhaps. If you consider Coventry City Football Club's recent performance "warlike". It was their emblem, twisted around his bulging deltoids. Hence my getting the two lads talking about their Christmas boxes – their accents confirmed it. You saw how irritated he was when they spoke.'

'I did!'

'So then – find a thriving male gymnasium in the Coventry area with a history of supplying heavies to local security firms, and by a few careful inquiries, we can discover the identity of our "Zabkus". His name is Lee Sopwell, a common-or-garden supplier of stolen goods who's somehow stumbled into the big time.'

'Bravo, Holmes!'

19

Holmes was by now halfway through his fillet steak and waving at the waiter to keep filling his glass of claret to the brim.

'Much to my disappointment,' Holmes said, 'it turns out he was being honest. He *doesn't* know who his supplier of rare jewels is. Which is why I was glad to have grappled his mobile telephone in that way for some helpful information. A convincing performance, I thought?'

'Very,' I agreed.

'While pretending to fumble with the buttons, in a trice I looked at the most recent Google Map locations Zabkus/Sopwell had searched for. So there I went to *explore* in the working-class environs of North London. You know full well, Watson, I can slip easily into the lower echelons of society. Being a natural man of the people, of course, I understand life on the streets. I say, the decor of the Garrick really is going downhill these days, isn't it. Can't these halfwits manage a lick of Farrow & Ball once in a while?'

'I hadn't noticed,' I confessed. 'It seems as opulent to me as ever . . .'

'Nonsense, it's practically falling apart. Is it too much to expect people to maintain standards? Well, let's leave this dump behind. We must venture to Islington – and visit the same address of one of Mr Zabkus's suppliers, which I plundered from his mobile device.'

'Now? But I've hardly—'

'Oh, you've had quite enough of that omelette. Beastly unhealthy things, didn't you know that? Waiter – call a cab at once . . . I've had enough of walking for one month, Watson . . . Yes, I'll have the rest of this bottle of red to go, thank you . . .'

'I am a man of the people, as you know, Watson. I say, isn't the Garrick's decor looking ghastly these days?'

20

Our taxi pulled up on a quiet, not to say economically distressed, backstreet in Islington. A cluster of children were kicking a ball against a garage door and a woman was shrieking at a dog as we approached Flat 55, Tennyson Mansions, a grimy brown-brick housing development.

The man who answered looked at us suspiciously, but when Holmes introduced himself, let us inside. He and his apartment were equally shabby and untidy, the air a thick blue gloom of half-dispersed cigarette smoke.

'I'm Jim Dellington, yes,' he said to Sherlock. 'I thought at first you two were police. Well, it's only a matter of time before they turn up. Could be any day.'

'So tell me,' said Sherlock, sitting at the kitchen table while Mr Dellington tucked his shirt into his trousers and poured an early afternoon measure of whisky into a 'BEST DAD EVER' mug. 'When did you start selling museum pieces?'

'About five years ago,' he said. 'You see, when I started at the museum in 1995, I was over the moon. I always worshipped it when I was a child. To be surrounded by such artefacts – all day, every day!'

'And you were an archivist?' I asked.

'No, no, just a security guard. But you see, over the

years I started to realize what a terrible place it is, in many ways. The museum. All museums! These "finds" they have – some dug up by archaeologists, of course, but some bought from grave robbers and even warlords. And they just sit on them. For decade after decade. Not even looking at what they have. Just keeping them boxed up in darkness and silence – vaults of them, up and down the country – and only one per cent of the artefacts ever on display. I slowly started to be outraged by it.

'So I sold one online, to see what would happen. I didn't sleep for a week – but I didn't get arrested. The buyer was incredibly grateful; they were a researcher and couldn't believe their luck – it was a piece of Chinese pottery, from the Taklamakan Desert.'

'Then you started doing it regularly,' I said.

'And you sold some items directly to this fellow who calls himself "Zabkus",' said Holmes.

'That pillock. Yes, I did. Nothing too fancy – some Egyptian scroll fragments, some Bronze Age arrowheads. But he has his connections, and he pays. Listen,' he said, looking up at us both. 'My wife passed away last year. I used the money I made from selling artefacts to look after her. And now my kids are grown up, it doesn't matter what happens to me. In a way, I'm looking forward to this story coming out. The museum *deserves* the negative press – all they've done is take these items and deliberately hidden them for fifty years! If I go to prison in order to expose what a sham they are, it will be worthwhile. Now, if you gentlemen will excuse me, there's a documentary I want to watch . . . I do love history, you see . . .'

His drink slopped on his clothes as he sat heavily on his settee and switched on the television.

'. . . now *here* was someone Catherine the Great wasn't going to kick out of bed for farting . . .' intoned Akila Jassim, beaming brightly from the square in front of the St Petersburg Hermitage.

Holmes and I let ourselves out.

'So, Watson,' said Holmes, when we had returned to Baker Street. 'We are at a dead end with Zabkus/Sopwell.'

'Which sounds like some kind of skin condition,' I said.

'Indeed. With the same symptoms as being in decidedly hot water, I imagine. The law won't be long in catching up with both of them. Now, I'm hoping that there will be a prearranged signal . . . Yes! There it is!'

Holmes had been peering out of the window, scouring the street for some sign. On seeing it, to my amazement, this cunning master of disguise, concealment and every kind of secret code now stood up straight and waved both hands cheerfully over his head.

'How marvellous! Watson, I would like you to meet someone very dear to me.'

There was a discreet knock at the door, and in walked a young woman.

After a long history of describing my encounters with new people, I have recently been made aware (by my great-niece) of certain changes in etiquette. Most particularly, that it is not entirely appropriate behaviour by a man of certain years to talk enthusiastically (as I have on many occasions in the past) about the physical beauty of young women. This is only one narrow aspect of a whole human being, after all.

With this in mind I say that the person who then entered the room had undoubtedly a most *striking* appearance, and her visual aspect made a strong impression upon me. She was perhaps twenty years old, and came to sit beside Sherlock Holmes with an ease and familiarity that showed they were already old friends.

'Watson, while I was undercover exploring the crime-ridden cesspits of the Borough of Hackney – but also drinking some very delicious coffee, I admit – I could not continue all my researches alone. Therefore I took it upon myself to engage an intern. And – in turn – here she is!'

'Most delighted, young lady,' I said, reaching out my hand.

'Not supposed to call a young woman "lady" these days, Watson,' muttered Holmes quietly.

'Well, *woman* then – or, *person* – ah, excuse me . . .'

'I'm Chichima,' she said. 'It's so nice to meet you. I sent a letter to Mr Holmes saying I wanted to help in any way, because I'm a bit of a fangirl of you two. I couldn't believe when he actually accepted my offer of assistance . . .'

'No one else ever offered before!' Holmes said. 'Chichima has been helping me with some research. But please – I'll let you tell us . . .'

She smiled, and took out a notebook. 'It's taken quite a lot of digging,' she said. 'And careful questioning. But here we go. The man run over three years ago on the sixth of December in Russell Square was called Chin Hua Huang. He was a teacher. Married with no children. He was killed just a few yards from the Museum of Antiquities. The next year, Rutvi Shetty fell under the eastbound Piccadilly line train at South Kensington station. Just round the corner from the blockbuster exhibition of African art that was on at that time. And last year Etera Henare, of Maori descent, was found dead in the river. We don't know where he could have been. But possibly in the vicinity of a museum displaying some artefact that would connect to our others.'

'Wonderful work!' I applauded.

'And our recent victim?' asked Holmes.

'Our latest corpse, from two weeks ago, is James Cadogan, a Scottish gentleman. Who just so happens to have an Ethiopian mother, and to have grown up largely in Ethiopia.'

'Tell us about these men,' said Holmes. He was leaning back and had adopted a thoughtful attitude, his eyes on the ceiling.

'They were all in the same class at the School of Oriental and African Studies, thirty years ago. They were in attendance at a famous lecture where one of their professors asked his students to assemble a list of the most grievous cultural thefts still linked to British museums. Aside from the very famous ones – the Rosetta Stone, the Elgin Marbles, the Benin Bronzes and so forth. These were the less famous ones, but no less insulting and crucial to the peoples who had lost them. After much discussion they came up with a list of nine. The "SOAS treasures", they were nicknamed – and all of them precious jewels. News of this found its way into the right-wing media, there was a fuss – and the professor lost his job. The entire class was discontinued, in fact.'

'This list . . .' I began.

Chichima nodded. 'It contained the Baghdad Beryl and the Lucknow Teardrop.'

Holmes uttered a growl of satisfaction. 'Now we're *getting* somewhere . . .' he said.

22

'After the professor's firing,' Chichima went on, 'there was a backlash – insofar as students were able to generate such things before social media. There was rumoured to be a group who vowed to take revenge against the establishment for these crimes – a society for the repatriation of precious artefacts. They determined to work their whole lives to make sure this historical injustice was redressed.

'The injustice of culturally stolen art in general?' Holmes asked. 'Or these SOAS treasures in particular?'

'I imagine they wanted to redress as many instances as they could,' Chichima said. 'But this SOAS case was definitely their particular obsession. Henare became an academic, Chin Hua a teacher, Mr Shetty worked in the museum trade for a long while, James Cadogan was a journalist. They used to meet in an upstairs room at a pub in East London to discuss how their efforts were getting on. But despite everything, after nearly three decades, they were no closer to getting the outcome they desired. That is, through legal means.'

'The treasures were still here,' said Holmes.

Chichima nodded. 'The museums made vague noises about agreeing to some of their demands, but in reality stood fast. And it seems possible that gradually, despairing of success, they started to think of a more adventurous and direct way of repatriating these things.'

'And more deadly!' said I.

'That's *exactly* the point,' said Holmes. 'I suspected all along that some sort of group like this was at work – although the Santa connection still mystifies me. And more than that – the *murderousness*. The whole establishment was arranged against them, and they were committing crimes. Why not have the blighters locked up and return the artefacts to the museums? It doesn't make sense! There is something still to be discovered in all this . . .'

Chichima spoke up. Her eyes were twinkling. 'That's not all,' she said. 'From what I've heard about the original group, there was a fifth member: in fact, the ringleader. Their identity was a very closely guarded secret. So there could be one secret Santa still out there, yet to be killed in the commission of a burglary.'

'And that person holds the final secrets and will be able to tell us all!' said Holmes.

23

'I don't see at all why it is necessary to accost me in this way,' said Lord Winterbourne. 'Explain yourselves!'

'My dear sir,' said Sherlock Holmes. 'There has been a breakthrough in your case which I must discuss with you.'

'Couldn't you contact me during business hours?' he asked. 'I thought I was dealing with professionals.'

'I perceive you are embarrassed to be accosted in a branch of Ann Summers,' Holmes airily suggested.

'But I deleted those tweets years ago!'
'Nothing is ever truly deleted on the internet, sir,' said Holmes.

'For God's sake, let's go outside,' said the flustered peer of the realm.

'Really, I see nothing to be embarrassed about, in this day and age,' said Holmes once we were on the pavement. 'Unless it is that Ann Summers's stock is dreadfully out of date – only for hen parties and middle-aged account managers. To find items really suited to an intimate partner you should be looking at specialist online shops . . .'

'You certainly seem to know a lot about it,' said Winterbourne, striding quickly along the street towards the blanketing shadows of Soho.

'Not at all,' said Holmes, easily matching his pace. 'I suggest you take on a young intern, you might learn a few things. For instance, that the Oxford Street branch of Ann Summers is the inevitable destination of an older man with a younger mistress who rapidly has to get her a present.'

'If you say so,' hissed Lord W. 'It must be Friday again, I see – for have your idiot cousin in tow.'

'What does he mean, Holmes?' I asked loudly and with studied innocence, as we went along. Holmes shot me a warning glance which read: *don't overdo it.*

Uttering a final grunt of disgust, Winterbourne turned in at a bar door and found a distant corner table in the Pillars of Hercules. He sat with his back to the room, betraying every sign of nervous distraction, while Holmes ordered drinks.

'Now, what do you want?' Winterbourne asked when we were all at the table. He glanced nervously over his shoulder as our drinks were brought over by the barman, and held his glass up suspiciously.

'Why do you keep giving me brandy and soda? Who do you think I am, Bertie Wooster? For goodness' sake, barman, a pint of lager, if you please. Thank you. Now, Holmes, I hope you can explain yourself.'

'I most certainly can,' said Sherlock Holmes. 'My only hope is that you can do the same in return.'

And so Holmes began.

24

When Holmes's explication of the story, so far as he had been able to put it together, came to an end, Winterbourne was a different person.

Gone was the domineering and all-powerful figure we had first met. In his place was a hunted creature, someone who had come face to face with a terrible spectre from his past.

He slurped down his brandy and soda in one gulp, then sat brooding over his pint of Dortmunder.

'I didn't think you'd get to the heart of it so soon,' he said quietly. 'I am ... reluctantly impressed by your skill. What you suggest ... well, let me tell it from the start.'

'I wish you would,' said Holmes.

'There was a very powerful man in museum circles, once,' Winterbourne said. 'He is dead now, and his name is unimportant – although you can guess it easily enough. He was above all us others, and we revered him. Quite wrongly, as it turned out. He was compromised in his private life, and had been blackmailed for years. To meet the demands of his blackmailers, he had made a copy of a very valuable piece of jewellery which was in his trust, and had sold the real jewel. It might not have been discovered for fifty or a hundred years – if it wasn't for this damned SOAS business.'

'It was one of the gems on the famous list,' said Holmes.

Winterbourne nodded, looking tired. 'Those nine SOAS treasures all happen to be precious pieces of jewellery. With extraordinary resale value on the black market. After the story of the fired professor blew up, and everyone was suddenly talking about these treasures, one of them was inspected and found to be a fake. We confronted the man responsible, and he confessed. The original was long gone. Above everything else we stood for in the museum community, this was unconscionable. Museums are supposed to keep artefacts safe, that's their most basic responsibility!

'There was a great soul-searching among us. And we found – it was just too embarrassing for it to come out. We decided we must gather round him to help.'

'To help?' I asked. 'How?'

'You mean, to cover it up,' said Holmes.

'To prevent total humiliation of Britain as a bastion of cultural heritage,' Lord Winterbourne said testily. 'The SOAS thing, and all the movements to repatriate cultural treasures, they caught us off guard. I don't disagree with them! Of course one can see they are right. It's a disgrace that we have refused to admit to the injustice of it all.'

'The Elgin Marbles,' suggested Holmes.

'Yes. And the Rosetta Stone,' said Winterbourne, taking a sip. 'Whatever right have we to that? It belongs in Egypt!'

'The Benin Bronzes,' I put in.

'Indeed,' he said, then shot me a mildly sceptical look as I realized I had betrayed my supposed intellectual status. But his thoughts quickly got back on track.

'We just did not have it in us to confess what had happened. That one of the world's great artworks had been stolen and replaced with a fake – and *by someone within the museum community* – was the worst of all worlds. So, yes – we covered it up.'

Holmes was looking at him with profound concentration. The unlit pipe was in his mouth, his teeth practically grinding it to dust. He sensed – as I perceived – that we were close to the centre of the mystery.

'It was agreed,' said Lord Winterbourne, 'that the eight remaining jewels should be withdrawn, and replaced with excellent replicas, and put in a place of absolute safety, entrusted to one person. So nothing like this could occur again.'

Grind, grind, went Holmes's teeth against the bone stem of his pipe.

'But you – a very senior member of this exclusive group of museum curators – did not yourself know where the hiding place was,' Holmes said.

'I did not.'

'And all of a sudden a few weeks or months ago you became desperate to know this hiding place. You were afraid. You said to your wife, if only I could hold in my hand the Baghdad Beryl. We have spoken to your wife, by the way, during our investigations – fear not, she suspects nothing.'

'You are correct – I suddenly felt an overwhelming need to know where it was hidden.'

'Therefore,' Sherlock said, 'you suspected that some nefarious activity was going on. Perhaps it had come to your attention that another fake had come on the market. Perhaps the person you entrusted the jewels to was showing more and more erratic behaviour, and making you nervous. *Perhaps* – and you don't have to answer this – you were aware that several people had been killed. Killed very near to museums displaying (or pretending to display) gems from this very list.'

Winterbourne had recovered some of his composure. He met Holmes's eye levelly.

'I receive briefings about serious crimes from the Metropolitan Police as a matter of course,' he said.

Holmes nodded. 'Naturally. You are on the House of Lords Serious Crime and Police Committee. Perhaps the police didn't understand the crimes, but you put two and two together. And all of a sudden became *afraid* that the person who took control of those jewels *in the public interest* had become a rogue agent . . . capable of murder . . .'

25

'I can say no more,' said Winterbourne, leaping up. 'My time is precious. When I approached you it was in the hope that you could return the jewel to me, nothing more. I did not intend that all this should come to light. This villain Zabkus . . .'

'Is innocent,' said Sherlock. 'In this matter, that is. Despite his other criminality. As a matter of fact, the man's name is Sopwell. From Coventry.'

Winterbourne nodded distractedly and gathered up his bag of lingerie.

'Send me your bill,' he said. 'I shall settle it at once. I don't want to hear from you again.'

'I shall do so,' said Holmes. 'But may I make a suggestion?'

Winterbourne turned a harassed and sarcastic gaze on Holmes at this final parley.

'Your wife is a kind and thoughtful woman who loves you more than anything in the world. Which cannot be said of your girlfriend. Who is she, may I ask?'

'You overstep the mark, sir. Perhaps you think I am a foolish old man secretly keeping some dancing girl in a flat in Camberwell, like a cheap 1930s novel. I assure you she is a highly distinguished intellectual and translator.

Ask Sir Gerald Huntingdon, no less – he *begged* her to work on this new exhibition of his . . .'

He broke off, realizing he'd said too much, and a moment later was out of the door, which slammed behind him.

Silence hung over our table for a moment, and the background buzz of the public house soothed our questioning thoughts.

'I do think he is a fool, as a matter of fact,' Holmes admitted. 'But my rather childish ruse paid off – that final comment was most instructive.'

'Where is all this going, Holmes?' I asked. 'I must admit, I am enthralled!'

'Where exactly, cousin, I do not know. But there are a few secrets yet to be revealed. Now finish your brandy and pootle off to Baker Street, would you? It's shop o'clock and Santa's got a secret gift to purchase.'

There was a brief pause, and we looked at each other.

'No, rest assured, *not* at Ann Summers,' he said, and we both burst out laughing.

Having completed my 10,000 steps for the day I decided
to catch the Number 38 bus home – only to find it was
utterly full.

26

'Today's the day, Watson, today's the day,' Holmes said. He was carefully tying a bow tie in the mirror, and tutting as his fingers fumbled the knot. In front of him on the mantelpiece stood our invitation to the opening of the latest Museum of Great Britain exhibition: 'Achaemenid Empire: Moment of Destiny'.

'I can't deny I am *nervous*!' Holmes said. 'Where's Chichima?'

'Here,' said the young woman, who had been hard at work at her laptop on the sofa.

'I don't suppose you would help me with this?' he asked. She looked at it, and saying she didn't know what or why it was, refused.

'Besides, I've got to go,' she said. 'I start my shift at Domino's in fifteen.'

'I thought you were at university, young lady – I mean, woman?'

'Yes, but I've also got three jobs. University is expensive. Good luck today. It sounds sick,' she said.

'Sick?' said Holmes. 'You mean I seem unwell? Or there is something ill-omened about the event?'

Chichima sighed patiently.

'Ah!' said Holmes. 'I deduce this is a slang term. You mean that today's events should turn out not "sick" but indeed "healthy",' he deduced. 'I hope you are indeed right, but I confess I have some serious doubts . . .'

'Thanks, Sherlybaby,' she said, admiring his completed bow tie over his shoulder in the mirror and removing a spot of lint from his collar. 'You're absolutely killing it right now.'

Holmes, never shy of praise, let out a sigh of satisfaction. 'As long as "it" remains the only thing that is killed today,' he said. 'Which makes me think. Before you go — both of you. Why Santa?'

'Holmes?' I asked.

'Why did this group, who all grew up chafing under the aegis of the British Empire, choose Santa as their emblem?'

'I don't hold with this "Santa" business,' I said. 'Beastly Americanism! He's Father Christmas, to be sure!'

'It *does* seem a weird costume to adopt while protesting against Western cultural oppression,' Chichima said.

Holmes spun to look at us both. I could see at once he was pleased with himself and had something to say, so I took his place in front of the mirror to attempt to tie my own bow.

'Saint Nicholas,' he said. 'Died in Myra, in the fourth century. At the time, Myra was in the Roman Empire. Yet this saint — who loved giving gifts to children — over the years became the patron saint of the midwinter festival in many European countries. Gifts were given in his name.'

I saw Chichima checking the time on her phone.

'It is only in the eighteenth and nineteenth centuries

that Saint Nicholas's fame is taken away and given to Jesus. Gift-giving moves to the twenty-fifth of December. He is still called "Sinterklaas" in some places, but in others this is replaced by a rather general and vague gift-giving spirit – "Father Christmas", "Père Noël" and so on – an anodyne facsimile of the traditional meaning.

'And what happened to his remains? They were *dug up and stolen* by Christian Crusaders, removed from Myra and taken to Bari in Italy, where they are now – despite multiple requests for their return. And do you know, Bari receives lots of visitors on pilgrimage to see his remains. So Santa Claus himself is a stolen relic, and a tourist attraction! What do you think of that?'

I was still struggling to get my bow tie to assemble, and unable for a moment to respond.

'An example of complex cultural influences, to be sure . . .' I said.

'And where is Myra, deathplace of Saint Nicholas? In the Achaemenid Empire! No wonder I'm looking forward to getting a look at this exhibition!'

27

'The other reason Santa was a good choice,' Holmes whispered to me as we approached the Museum of Great Britain and saw the impressive lights playing across its vast frontage, 'is more commonsensical.'

'I thought of that too,' I said. 'If one wants to go about London in a disguise during the Christmas party season, what could be more concealing and yet more natural?'

'Exactly, Watson! Yes, thank you – here are our passes,' Holmes said to the burly security guard by the door.

We were allowed in with a drifting crowd of well-dressed and rather impressive-looking people, offered a glass of champagne on a silver platter, and then we were in the Grand Exhibition Room, which we had last seen under such very different circumstances.

'How did they hush this up, Holmes?' I said. 'Surely it's a scandal that this room was so recently a murder scene . . .'

'They've not proved it was murder – and I don't think they even think that it is, as yet . . .' As he spoke he nodded at Inspector Kanchelsky across the room. She was looking decidedly uncomfortable in a tuxedo, and casting suspicious glances at the crowd of elderly and visibly wealthy museum patrons and donors.

'Why are we here, Holmes?' I asked.

'Well, aside from my sincere interest in the Achaemenid Empire, and the fact that I've never been invited to one of these shindigs before, I've had a small realization that will make for a decidedly interesting conversation with the museum's curator, Sir Gerald. He has some particularly difficult questions to answer.'

'Ladies and gentlemen,' said a voice as the lights dimmed. 'Please bring your hands together for the curator of the Museum of Great Britain, Sir Gerald Huntingdon . . .'

Loud applause filled the dark room, and into a spotlight in the centre moved a recognizable figure – like Holmes and myself, spruced to the nines and wearing a black dinner jacket. He held up a hand and the room hushed.

'This is a very exciting moment for me, and for the museum,' he said. 'I am thrilled to welcome you all here and to introduce this major and distinctly magical exhibition. But now,' he checked his watch, 'something even more special. You see, I have to be very precise with the time . . . Lights please!'

A screen lit up behind him, showing the sun setting over a distant horizon.

'That is the sun setting over the Iranian plateau,' he

said into his microphone. 'Our exhibition – "Moment of Destiny" – is named for the Achaemenid crowning ceremony, performed annually at sunset on the winter solstice – which is in just a few moments. When the new leader accepts the crown . . .'

There was a reverent silence as he held up an ancient headpiece, of carefully detailed gold with a bright jewel in its centre. Beneath the bright lights the multifaceted gem winked at the entire hushed assembly.

Beside me, I sensed Sherlock Holmes growing tense.

'What's this . . .' he muttered.

On the screen, the final sliver of the setting sun lingered hazily.

'And so, by becoming the first person to perform this ritual in perhaps two thousand years, I create continuity with this ancient and wonderful civilization, bringing it to life in more ways than one . . .'

'No!' yelled Holmes. He sprang forward into the crowd, and there were murmurs and angry comments as he tried to get through the assembled dignitaries.

'Stop!' Holmes shouted. I was afraid he had gone out of his senses, and had no idea what I ought to do. I half wanted to reach my friend and drag him back, but it was too late and he had always been far more athletic than myself.

Sherlock Holmes reached the side of the stage as the crown touched Sir Gerald's pate, and a beatific smile, or perhaps a smile of glorying in power, spread across his face. He was utterly oblivious to the interruption.

Then a bloodcurdling scream ripped through the air. It came from the museum curator's mouth. One moment he was standing and beaming with self-importance.

The next he was curled on the floor, writhing.

In the instant before pandemonium broke out, I was able to get a glimpse of him in the gap left by Holmes's desperate bid to save his life.

The man's face was utterly withered and transfixed by a look of total horror. Trickles of blood came from his mouth, nose, ears and eyes.

The writhing stopped, and he lay lifeless. A wisp of smoke rose from around the crown.

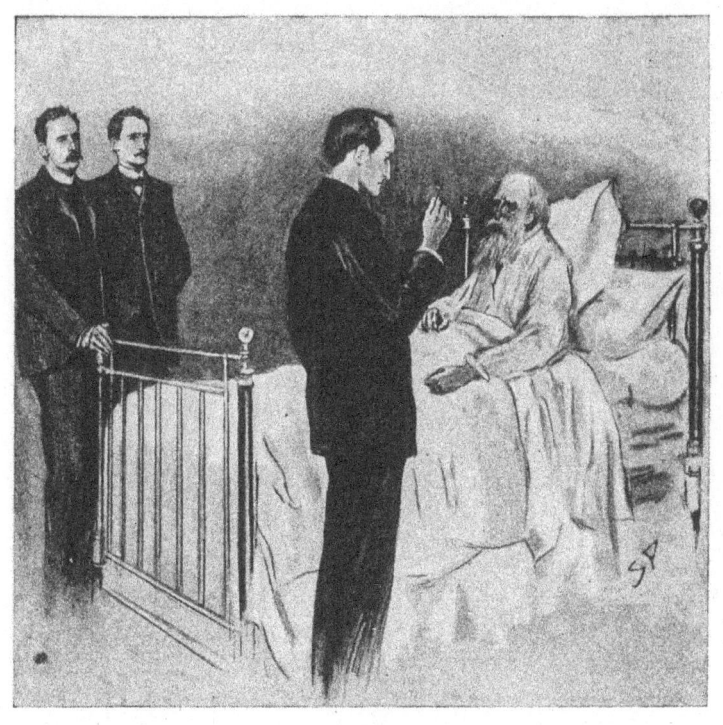

'How long was I in a coma – I haven't missed my GCSEs, have I?'
'Mr Halliwell, I'd like you to prepare yourself to receive some bad news . . .'

28

It took only a few minutes for the whole audience to be marshalled out of the room. Emergency services ran back and forth, and panic of a very British and well-behaved sort reigned – but panic nevertheless.

'Holmes,' I said, as I saw my friend walking towards the street. 'The police will want to speak to us! They asked us all to stay in place!'

'Nonsense,' he said. 'They've got all our names, have they not? We had to sign in after all. I'm going for a drink.'

I sensed that he was keen to avoid the well-dressed gossipy rabble who were gathering and discussing what they had seen, not to mention the many journalists present who were swarming among them like sharks at feeding time.

'I shall have a sherry,' said Holmes, after wrestling his way to the bar of the pub opposite. Having escaped the museum crowd, we were still in a Central London pub just a few days before Christmas. The pervading atmosphere of shouting and merry-making made it hard to think, and I struggled to stay by the side of my friend in the pressing morass.

'Why, if it isn't the famous detective,' said a voice. In the melee it was hard to make out, but I thought I noticed both fondness and gentle mockery in the tone.

Holmes and I both turned, and found ourselves face to face with the dazzling smile of the TV historian Akila Jassim.

'Ms Jassim,' said Holmes severely. 'I am in no mood for your jocular antics. I take it you were in the room with us just now and saw what happened?'

'Yes,' she said. Her smile did not waver. 'Beastly business, as you would probably say. Ghastly. *Dastardly!* Who could have predicted it?' The barman supplied her with a pint of Guinness and she sipped it demurely, looking up at Holmes with wide eyes. I could not in that moment decide whether to take her attitude as impish and humorous or (in the light of what we had all witnessed just minutes earlier) deplorably inhumane.

'You don't like me, Mr Holmes,' she suggested.

'I don't see why a superlatively talented woman such as yourself should pretend to be so stupid and facile in your public persona, I confess,' he said imperiously.

She shrugged, and still smiling, took another sip of her drink and looked around at the throng. 'I want to get ahead in life, and I'm doing it the best way I can.'

'But someone with your talents,' Holmes protested. 'Someone who Sir Gerald *begged* to help him translate the materials for the Achaemenid exhibiton . . .'

She raised an eyebrow.

'I think you understood perfectly what was going to happen when he put on that crown. Or suspected at least. Because it was not a crown at all, was it? Quite the opposite. An artefact which generates intense power, and transmits it inwards with huge concentration. A device for cooking the brain. One might almost say—'

Akila Jassim laughed brilliantly. 'I see what you're getting at. It's like an ancient air fryer! Wouldn't catch me using one of those things. Full-fat chips for this girl.'

'You admit it?' I asked.

'What can I say? Even experts make mistakes,' she said. 'I translated the name of the ceremony as the "Moment of Destiny", but exact translation isn't always possible. Perhaps the word might better be rendered as "fate", "peril" or "doom". What occurred was a most terrible accident.'

I saw Holmes's mind working fast. 'You knew Sir Gerald had worked at all the other museums where your confrères, the other secret Santas, had tried to retrieve famous gems. He had the jewels sequestered and was selling convincing fakes of them on the black market to line his own pockets. It was easily done – he knew wealthy and interested collectors, and allowed them to catch wind that the ones on display were fakes. He, of course, had been involved in commissioning the "original" fakes – if that isn't too confusing a phrase – in the first place, and could get more made. He also happened to be a narcissist and a psychopath – prepared to kill to avoid being exposed . . .'

'It's an interesting theory,' she said. 'You *are* clever. Tell me more!'

'What I don't understand is why James Cadogan was at the museum in the first place, in order to get murdered,' Holmes said, thinking to himself. Akila watched

97

him as he made his deductions, her eyes twinkling. 'I suspect he'd worked out that this particular jewel had to be used in the exhibition. Perhaps he acted rashly, without your approval. You were the ringleader of the group, after all – you were not in that famous class at SOAS, because we checked the register, but I realize now you were of course at the school at the time, and must have snuck in.

'The previous thefts all took place on the sixth of December, the feast day of Saint Nicholas. But when you made the translations, you knew this later date, when the crown was activated, would be much more propitious.'

'And deadly!' said I.

'With Cadogan's unfortunate death, you knew for sure the identity of the killer. And you knew he would not reveal the true hiding place of the gems except when *forced* to produce one of them – at an event which required one of the genuine jewels to be used, for absolute authenticity. He was so narcissistic he could not resist the opportunity you gave him. You watched his movements carefully, and discovered the location where he had concealed all the jewels. And at last it was the gem's very authenticity which killed him!'

'If what you say is true,' Akila Jassim said, 'it's hardly a fair trade, is it, one life in return for the four he took? According to your theory, that is.'

'And you strung Lord Winterbourne along to try to get hold of the real gems, until you realized he could only supply you with fakes, despite he and his wife both impoverishing themselves for the same sorry purpose.'

Her look hardened. 'I don't know his wife,' she said. 'If that is true I'm very unhappy to hear it. But as I say. An interesting theory. It's been nice having a drink with you, Sherlock Holmes,' she said, putting her glass on the bar between the jostling bodies of London drinkers urgently placing their orders. 'You didn't disappoint,' she said. And, favouring him with a saucy wink, she pulled on a Santa hat.

'What are you going to do now?' Holmes asked.

'Well, my new documentary is in the bag,' she said.

'What's it called?' asked Holmes. '*Alexander the Great-in-the-Sack?*'

'Wait and see,' she said, and blessed him with another one of her lascivious winks. 'It airs in the spring. I know a fan when I see one. Before then, I'm going on a little holiday. To Baghdad, to Lucknow, and then on to six other places . . .'

Before Holmes or I could open our mouths, she had melted into the crowd, her hand subtly but tightly clutching her shoulder bag.

29

Christmas morning had come and gone. Between the Christmas cards on the mantelpiece were two empty stockings. On top of one lay a pristine moustache comb, and on the other a pair of brand-new brown woollen socks (extra-coarse).

'I tell you for the thousandth time, Watson,
I have no need for reading glasses.'

What's more, two identical large boxes stood in the corner of the room, signifying that the annual present-giving ceremony had provided the household with not one but two air fryers.

'Dinner nearly ready, Watson?' Holmes carolled from the next room. I called back in the affirmative.

'Table is set!' he said.

I had discovered in the few hours that I had been exposed to its workings that the Air Fryer Multi-Max 3000 was indeed a versatile machine, and a sequence of covered dishes were keeping warm. I hoped that there was room in the roof space for the second machine, alongside the rice cooker, bread maker, espresso machine and a dozen other gizmos left over from previous years, all untouched. In my flustered state I made a mental note to make a written note, to remind me to pay a trip to the charity shop in the new year.

'I'll get that!' said Holmes in response to a ring of the bell.

'Well well well, what do we have here then?' said a voice from the door.

'My goodness!' I said. 'Inspector Lestrade! As I live and breathe!'

'Doesn't he look awful,' said Holmes. 'You're ageing wretchedly, Inspector.'

'That's Mr Lestrade to you,' said Lestrade, accepting a glass of eggnog, sniffing it suspiciously and then set-tling into a chair. 'And speak for yourself, Holmes. You're no spring chicken.'

'Speaking of fowls, Watson, how goes the goose?' asked Holmes.

'All ready!' I said. The bell rang again. 'We're all set. Goodness, who can that be?'

'Merry Festivemas one and all,' said Chichima, coming in with a warm smile and handing over a package of Christmas crackers. 'Ah,' she said, seeing the air fryer boxes. 'Christmas AF.'

'Aldi's finest crackers!' said Holmes. 'Funny how they look identical to the Harvey Nicks ones, eh, Watson, only without that sticker strategically covering the brand name?'

'I, uh, don't know what you mean, Holmes . . .' I dithered.

'My dear fellow,' he said, clapping me on the back. 'I'm the world's greatest detective, in case you'd forgotten. Besides, I think I prefer the Tesco Christmas pud to the Fortnum's one. I am a man of the people, after all, as I was telling you the other day.'

'What's on telly later?' asked Lestrade, opening the *Radio Times* on his lap.

'There are certain traditions to be upheld,' said Holmes. 'The King's speech, then Wallace and Gromit, followed by *Elf*. Does that meet with your approval, my young friend?'

'Surely,' said Chichima. 'Although *Trading Places* was traditional holiday viewing in my home growing up. People forget that's a Christmas film.'

I saw an extra place set at table, and had a thought. 'Holmes, you set a place for Mrs Hudson!'

'Indeed – if you recall, she always falls out with her sister by Christmas morning and drives back in a terrible mood. She should be here in a few minutes – let's pour an eggnog for her.'

'Well remembered, Holmes,' I said. 'You are quite right. And of course Christmas isn't Christmas for dear Mrs H without her favourite Bruce Willis film . . .'

'Old habits die hard, Watson,' said Holmes, with a relaxed sigh. 'Now, if you will raise your glasses – Merry Christmas, one and all! And may all your cultural artefacts be returned to their place of origin!'

'Eh?' said Lestrade, wiping nog from his moustache.

'It's a long story,' I told him. 'Holmes – or should I call him Sherlybaby – will be delighted to elaborate . . .'

Thanks

I really love these short Holmes and Watson books, but they are written to tight deadlines and I rely a lot on friends and loved ones for advice. It would be unspeakably rude for me not to thank those who've helped: Shyam Kumar and Max Edwards first, as editor and agent. Then Steve Savage, who in my mind is uncredited co-author for all his brilliant ideas, and Mara Livermore for giving specialist museum help. Also Evelyn Conn and Kate Hooper. Sally Dolton always deserves thanks for generalized pervasive supportiveness. As do Catharine and Roger Vincent.

This little book is dedicated with immense gratitude and affection to Sara O'Keeffe.